ELMO'S LITTLE GLOWWORM

Featuring Jim Henson's Sesame Street Muppets

by **Elizabeth Rivlin**
Illustrated by **Joe Mathieu**

How to use this Glowback™ book:
The pages in this book have been printed with a nontoxic phosphorescent ink that glows in the dark. When you see the ⋆, turn off the lights—and you'll see the glowworm! Then turn the lights back on and continue reading.

Random House 🏠 New York

Library of Congress Cataloging-in-Publication Data: Elmo's little glowworm / illustrated by Joe Mathieu p. cm. SUMMARY: Elmo looks in Count's castle, Oscar's trash can, Big Bird's nest, and other places on Sesame Street before he finds his little glowworm in time for bed. ISBN 0-679-85402-9
1. Glow-in-the-dark books—Specimens. [1. Puppets—Fiction. 2. Glow-in-the-dark books. 3. Toy and movable books.] I. Mathieu, Joseph, ill. II. Title: Elmo's little glowworm. PZ7.E4798 1994 [E]—dc20 93-38193

Manufactured in Taiwan 10 9 8 7 6 5 4 3 2 1

Elmo had a little glowworm. He showed it to all his friends on Sesame Street.

"Glow, little glowworm," he said. He was so proud!

Then one day Elmo's little glowworm crawled away.

Elmo went to look for his little glowworm. He looked
in Oscar-the-Grouch's trash can.

Elmo found one old sneaker, a torn magazine, and
a sardine sandwich.

But no little glowworm.

Can you see Elmo's little glowworm?★

Elmo went to the playground to look for his little glowworm.

He looked on top of the slide and under the seesaw.

He crawled inside the barrel.

"Are you there, Little Glowworm?"

Elmo's voice echoed back to him. It sounded VERY LOUD!

He jumped out of that barrel fast!

Where is Elmo's little glowworm?★

Elmo went to Hooper's Store to look for his little
glowworm.

He looked on every shelf and behind the counter.

But Elmo found no little glowworm.

Then he opened the door to the storage room.

Out fell a mop, a bucket, and two brooms!

"Okey-dokey," said Elmo. "I guess Elmo's glowworm's
not in there."

Where is he?★

Elmo went to Hooper's Store to look for his little glowworm.

He looked on every shelf and behind the counter.

But Elmo found no little glowworm.

Then he opened the door to the storage room.

Out fell a mop, a bucket, and two brooms!

"Okey-dokey," said Elmo. "I guess Elmo's glowworm's not in there."

Where is he?★

Elmo went to the Count's castle to look for his little glowworm.

It was dark and spooky in the castle hall.

A bat flapped by Elmo's head.

A black cat streaked between Elmo's legs.

The clock struck. Bong!

"Little Glowworm, are you here?" Elmo whispered.

"Ha, ha, ha! One, two, three—three scary things in the night!" cried the Count. "But no glowworm, my little friend."

Can you find Elmo's little glowworm?★

Elmo went to Big Bird's nest.
Big Bird was taking a nap.
Elmo tiptoed around him looking for his little
glowworm, but Big Bird woke up.
"I'm sure I didn't see any glowworm," said Big Bird.
Are you sure?
Look for Elmo's little glowworm.★

Elmo went to 1 2 3 Sesame Street.

He went into Ernie and Bert's bathroom to look for his little glowworm.

Elmo found Ernie's Rubber Duckie.

"Squeak, squeak!" said Elmo to Rubber Duckie. Rubber Duckie squeaked back.

Elmo helped Rubber Duckie swim in the sink.

He forgot all about his little glowworm.

Do you see Elmo's little glowworm anywhere?★

Finally, Elmo went to see if his little glowworm had
crawled home.

He looked behind the books in the bookcase.

He looked behind the big curtains in the living room.

He looked under the sofa and under the chairs. But
Elmo couldn't find that little glowworm anywhere!

Can you?★

Elmo was tired from searching for his little pet all day.
He climbed into his cozy bed and turned out the light.
And then Elmo saw his little glowworm glowing like
a night-light on the wall!
"Glow, little glowworm," said Elmo, and fell asleep.★